To my own sweet little Viking. This story is for you. Love always, Mama —A.P.

To all the (not-quite) littlest Vikings everywhere, especially those whose thrones have been usurped by the wee ones —I.R.

THIS IS A BORZOI BOOK PUBLISHED BY ALFRED A. KNOPF

Text copyright © 2018 by Alexandra Penfold

Jacket art and interior illustrations copyright © 2018 by Isabel Roxas

All rights reserved. Published in the United States by Alfred A. Knopf, an imprint of Random House Children's Books, a division of Penguin Random House LLC, New York.

Knopf, Borzoi Books, and the colophon are registered trademarks of Penguin Random House LLC.

Visit us on the Web! randomhousekids.com

Educators and librarians, for a variety of teaching tools, visit us at RHTeachersLibrarians.com

Library of Congress Cataloging-in-Publication Data
Names: Penfold, Alexandra, author. | Roxas, Isabel, illustrator.
Title: The littlest Viking / by Alexandra Penfold ; illustrated by Isabel Roxas.
Description: First edition. | New York : Alfred A. Knopf, 2018. | Summary: "The littlest Viking must deal with an even littler Viking—his new baby sister." —Provided by publisher
Identifiers: LCCN 2017022324 (print) | LCCN 2016047301 (ebook) | ISBN 978-0-399-55431-5 (ebook) | ISBN 978-0-399-55429-2 (trade) | ISBN 978-0-399-55430-8 (lib. bdg.)
Subjects: | CYAC: Babies—Fiction. | Brothers and sisters—Fiction. | Vikings—Fiction.
Classification: LCC PZ7.1.P446 (print) | LCC PZ7.1.P446 Lit 2018 (ebook) |
DDC [E]—dc23

The text of this book is set in 18-point Dustismo.

The illustrations were created using gouache and colored pencils and dusted with digital magic dust.

MANUFACTURED IN CHINA

January 2018

10 9 8 7 6 5 4 3 2 1

First Edition

Random House Children's Books supports the First Amendment and celebrates the right to read.

THE LITTLEST VIKING

By Alexandra Penfold

Illustrations by Isabel Roxas

Alfred A. Knopf · New York

Sven was the littlest Viking.

But that didn't matter.

He had the loudest cry . . .

the fiercest set of teeth . . .

. . . and if he felt like pillaging?

Well, let's just say no
one was bold enough
to stop him.

But what Sven loved
best were stories.

Sven could spend hours
listening to stories.
And in time . . .

. . . he learned to share them, too, telling tales of

heroes and battles,
ships and storms,

sea monsters and
ferocious beasts.

When Sven told
a story, all of
the other Vikings
stopped to listen.

Until, one day, no one had time for Sven's tales.
There was too much to do.
They were expecting someone special.

What's this? A fair maiden?

No, a warrior princess!

The warrior princess was little, but loud.
Very, very loud.

And sad. So, so sad.

She was not amused
by shiny plunder.

A ride on the great ship did not soothe her.

The skald's song only made her cry louder.

Sven knew what to do. He stepped up to her cradle and began to whisper.

The warrior princess was quiet for a moment. It was just enough time for Sven to begin his tale.

He told of a small, brave Viking
and a mighty warrior princess and
distant lands meant for exploring.

He told of fantastic voyages and
epic feasts and all the adventures
they would have.

"Good night, sweet princess,"
said Sven. "Tomorrow I will
tell you another story."

And so he did.

Sven was no longer the littlest Viking.
But that didn't matter. . . .

In fact, he didn't mind one bit.